John Huntley Skrine

Songs of the Maid

And Other Ballads and Lyrics

John Huntley Skrine

Songs of the Maid
And Other Ballads and Lyrics

ISBN/EAN: 9783744787369

Printed in Europe, USA, Canada, Australia, Japan

Cover: Foto ©Andreas Hilbeck / pixelio.de

More available books at **www.hansebooks.com**

SONGS OF THE MAID

And Other Ballads and Lyrics

BY

JOHN HUNTLEY SKRINE

AUTHOR OF 'JOAN THE MAID'
'COLUMBA,' ETC.

WESTMINSTER

ARCHIBALD CONSTABLE

AND CO. 1896

TO

MY WIFE

If carols to the Sun be due
  Who makes the throstle sing ;
If breath of flowers, whereon she blew,
  Be incense-breath to Spring ;
If faithful lyre forgets not who
  Taught passion to the string ;—
Dear Other heart in One, to you
  Love's singer-sheaf I bring.

CONTENTS

CONTENTS

CONTENTS

ANDREW LANG

' Not Shakespeare's self the play could frame
If the white Maid were heroine.'
Ah! say you?   We will mend our aim:
And since she walks the mortal scene
Too wonderful, nor art can fuse
Her starlight and our passion-hues,

We'll sing but how the star came nigher,
And how men saw it or how were blind,
How burned with fire of love or fire
Of anger, after each his kind.
The star's pure self who know not, know
Yet how the star-beam strikes below.

LOUIS' LOVE

LOUIS DE COUTES, PAGE OF JOAN

WHAT is this at Louis' heart
  Knocks amain?
Sweetness is it all or smart
  Pricks the vein,
Ever since from saddle-tree
Grave her glance commanded me
Loose her stirrup and let free
  Charger's rein?

'Twas as when our chief of dames,
  High Yolande,
'Mid her damsels' broidery frames
  Tall and bland,

3

SONGS OF THE MAID

Asked my name, and hearing sought,
Dreamer-like, some vanished thought,
Waking as to lips I caught
    White her hand.

Ah ! but that was Queen, and this
    Born how low !
Royal hand were hers to kiss
    Even so.
Where 's the queen so swift obeyed ;
Or shall ere, when all is said,
Lordlier mistress than the Maid
    Louis know ?

Is she beautiful ? I muse.
    Not as they
Whom the knights love.   Let them choose
    Whom they may :

LOUIS' LOVE

Though my years are now twice seven,
Saw I never under heaven
Such an awesome beauty leaven
    Limbs of clay.

'Tis not here and 'tis not there :
    None can tell
Why who names the Maiden fair
    Names her well.
Now it is her lightsome going,
Now the glory's overflowing
Out of deep eyes beyond knowing
    Strikes the spell.

There's a knight who turns and laughs
    Passing by ;
Names me with her as he quaffs,
    Winking sly.

Had this arm of mine the weight,
I would break the wanton's pate,
Daring breathe against her state
    Thoughts awry.

Sooth, I love, if heart-leaps are
    Signs thereof:
Yea, but as men love the star
    Throned above;
For, with virgin harness white,
She goes armoured-up in light,
Hardly more from reach of spite
    Than of love.

O she holds all men that be
    Wide apart.
'Tis as child she tenders me:
    There's the smart.

LOUIS' LOVE

Child! Yet I for her could hold
Banner till its lilies gold
Falling, wrapped in crimsoned fold
    Louis' heart.

Fie! in dreams again. And she
    Gave behest
I should wait her where the lea
    Ends to west.
Hist! I hear her coming, coming;
Hoof of blithe Rolande a-drumming
Loud on turf, my pulse bedumbing
    Loud in breast.

In five lengths of him or near
    She 'll to stand
Rein him: I shall take her spear
    Warm from hand:

She will drop, how soft, how keen !

See, the smile : and I, my queen,

Print the loyal kiss, unseen,

    On—Rolande.

THE BASQUE

THE BASQUE

STANDARD-BEARER TO JOAN AT ORLEANS

Oh, who is it giving the word to-day,
  Merry my mates, so shrewd?
'Be done with the oath, and be done with the
    play,
  And done with the roundel lewd,
And the joy-girls all of the camp shall pack':
  Now who is it rules so bold?
'Tis a maiden o' back of a destrier black,
  With a banner of lilies of gold.

Chorus

And it's O good-bye to my love so light,
  To the kiss and the arms entwining,

9

To the rouse and the roar and the riot o'
  night,
The roisterer's wooing, the wanton's flight:
For it's Up and after the Maid all white
  And the maiden banner shining.

Who is the Maid and what is her might
  To lord it o'er most and least,
Bidding lusty knight and soldier wight
  Be meek as the shaven priest?
Oh, she can teach us abide nor fly
  At the whang of a Godon's bow,
And a Frenchman look in an English eye
  And bandy buffet for blow.

Chorus

For it's Ho! and up to the rampart's jaws,
  In the sleet of the long-bow snowing:

THE BASQUE

It's Up and cut we the Lion his claws,
For their bills are reeds and their bolts are
    straws,
And their cannon a bluster of gusty flaws
Of a wind her banner up-blowing.

But hark ye well, 'tis the chaplain's bell,
   And the banner is dight for prayer :
The shrine is dressed, and the wine is blessed,
   And the body of God is there.
And the prayer she prayed is heard, I wist,
   For look on her, comrades mine,
How the Maid uprist with a beam of Christ
   In the grey, great eyes a-shine !

Chorus
Then it's Ho ! to the priest to be sained and
    shriven,
When the dawn of a fight is creeping.

For who will follow the Maid forgiven,

'Tis a helmet pricked or a corslet riven,

His bones to France and his soul to heaven,

And the Maid o'er a soldier weeping.

THOMAS DE COURCELLES

A JUDGE IN THE TRIAL OF JOAN

Jan. 14th, 1456, the night before his examination by
the Court of Rehabilitation

THEY call me greatest Doctor of our France.

  It may be so : for who were else to name ?

In learning ripest and in utterance.

  They say it, not I ; it is the world's acclaim.

They tell the mighty Past its Gerson well

Might own his after-self in our Courcelles.

It may be as they say it ; not for nought

    Have stars grown pale, watching my lamp and
      me

In the spring dawns of Paris ; and I wrought

  (God be my witness) not for place nor fee,

And scarce for praise. Men laughed, 'Our
    scholar's eyes
Still on his feet, howe'er that head may rise !'

Rise ! I am simple Canon ; shall be Dean
    One morn by act of time. My classmates own
Their mitres each. I grudge not, who have seen,
    Ranging the length of his worn Council down,
Eyes royal kindle, watchful how the wit
Of Thomas de Courcelles should fashion it.

I vowed my scholar soul from out herself
    Should flower, unmoulded of the windy world,
As on a stormless lap of mountain shelf
    No stately tree, but shapely, has unfurled
Her plenitude of bower and mellowing fruit.
Ha !—save a worm have bitten her at the root.

THOMAS DE COURCELLES

What will they question at their Board to-morrow,
   Brehal and the Archbishop? What's to know
From my lip more than other of the sorrow
   In luckless Rouen half a life ago?
Their trial could forgo me well, not miss;
Why waste a student's daylight over this?

All's known. Our Court made error. I was one.
   Yes, but the rawest. How should thirty year
Fetched from dim cloister into dazing sun
   Be wise 'gainst fifty in discerning her?
It was clerk hand they summoned, scholar head
In me. For judgment let them ask the dead.

God! if they only could! That *he* might stand
   Pale at their bar, tormented; he that lies
In Lisieux chantry,[1] safe, and overspanned
   With marbles of enshrining canopies.

[1] Bishop Cauchon, the presiding judge, was buried at Lisieux.

15

My chief, my curse, my devil; yea, that slew
This spirit's virgin honour, ere it knew.

He bade me write our sessions: cozeningly
   Pleaded my law-craft's service, eyed agloat
My first-wet sheets, 'for where in France as I
   So lucid scribe, so deft?'   I heard and wrote.
I wrote the death-writ of my peace.   That ink
The nightly poison-potion that I drink!

What is 't they work withal, these evil wills?
   I loved not,—loathed him; yet the insistent
      coil
Flattering enwound, a snake's caress that kills
   Like steel infrangible, more smooth than oil.
Now know I wherefore Satan was an asp—
Ah! men but learned the fang! I learn the clasp.

That once I fell, that once.   Shall all the story,
  Fair else, a flawless whole, by this be maimed?
Those shining days of Basle, the pleader's glory,
  Voice for our France prevailing, all defamed?
My house of life then on a tomb is built,
Her pleasant chambers spectre-plagued with guilt.

To-morrow!   'Tis the Court again.   And I
  Not justicer, but culprit.   How they'll look
As if they looked not, under eyebrow, shy,
  Feigning not think what think they must.   I
      brook
Scorn of eyes mortal, if but these be there:
But O, what eyes behind yon judge's chair!

Is this the hell of my misdoing?   SHE,
  She will be there, her eyes.   O God, my gaze

Might yet affront them, would they threaten me.
    But all in wonder, and a piteous daze
How hate should murder the meek love, they
    turn
Questioning on mine; and in their flame I burn.

ISABEAU D'ARC

MOTHER OF JOAN

After the Rehabilitation

Is she coming, sons, our maiden : is she coming ?
>   Long, so long
Grows it since they purged her wholly and the
>   King made right the wrong.

Would she tarry coming homeward ?   That were
>   not the girl we knew,
She so light of foot, no tarrier ever where was
>   help to do.

Changed? Oh yes, belike, among the soldiers
    and the princes there.
Yet our Margot at the Crowning found her the
    sweet child as e'er.

Ay, the prison, sooth, would change her, . . .
    and that wonder of the flame,
When it burnt not, and across it white and
    whole the Maiden came. . . .

Nay, what said I? Something wildered am I,
    and forget : for she
'Scapes at last; the Holy Father and the good
    King set her free.

Hark! the latch was lifted, was't not? and a
    step—so old I grow
One has fancies, hears or hears not, unlike others.
    Yet to know

Step of Joan at door, how could I fail it ?—no,
   for all the years—
Strong and light (ah! you remember) and a
   pleasure in the ears.

She will come.   But how to greet her, grown so
   wonderful and high,
Her that talks at ease with princes, walks with
   angels whispering nigh !

Nay, but she was wondrous always, and I saw it
   not, so blind ;
Loved her, chid her (yes, but seldom), like the
   rest of maiden-kind.

Like all maidens of all mothers, who should know
   her ?   Only sweet
More than others, only kinder : quicker fingers,
   gladder feet.

Who could find the angel in her, till the fire that
    let unfold
Dove wings on her as of silver and the feathers
    like to gold?

Who? For She, was't writ she knew Him, hers,
    for other than the rest,
Faint as all are from the womb nor dearer at the
    nursing breast?

Was there aught She marked in broadening limb
    and stature waxing tall,
Going, coming in, uprising, and downsitting like
    them all?

Then could I know mine, my wonder? Haply,
    shall I know her now,
If she comes with the white armour shining and
    the starry brow?

ISABEAU D'ARC

Nay, the russet kirtle, liker, as she wore it 'mong
the sheep.
'Dreaming': am I, sons? No matter. I am
heavy: let me sleep.

She will lift the latch, nor wake me: not at first.
But stooping there
I shall feel her through my dream by something
tender in the air.

Then a touch on this grey forehead: 'tis her lip.
A brightness grown
Over lids, until they open,—and the brightness
is my Joan.

PASQUEREL

CHAPLAIN OF THE MAID

In the silence where an old man lingers
   Faint of cheer and winter-white,
Shadows haunt me,—prince and chiefs and
     singers,
   Echoings of pomp and fight;
And the great Past's unforsaking fingers
Stay me faltering at the doors of night.

One there is, one shadow, never passes,
   Haunts downsitting and uprise,
Blends a toneless murmur with the masses
   And the chant's solemnities,
Or, in censer-fume upsoaring, glasses
Silver armour there and urgent eyes.

PASQUEREL

I am Pasquerel, of Joan the Maiden
    Priest and counsellor of soul,
Ere she mounted of the flesh unladen
    Homeward on the flame's uproll.
Days I lived in and the days I fade in,
Worth have only from her glory's dole.

Lo ! this wrinkled hand, it touched the wonder :
    Lo ! this hand, her worshipper's,
Touched in blessing ; and the dark brows under
    Thrilled it back with mystic stirs,
Seeing earth not holds and scarcely yonder
Hides wide heaven a pureness matching hers.

Yea, these ears have heard the breathings lowly,
    Where at edge of battle she
Laid from off the breast of her, the holy,
    Burden of her sins on me.

Shamed I heard and marvelling sore if wholly
Stainless might a soul and mortal be.

Mortal was she? verily, as in fashion?
    Ah! but if she were in sooth
Beam of Godhead born in clay to flash on
    Night of ours a dawn of truth,
Charioted aloft in fiery passion
Back from man's betrayal and his ruth!

Lo! they doomed the just one, and gainsayer
    None for the all-brave was bold.
Now they look on whom he burned, the slayer,
    And the friend on whom he sold:
Yea, for Holy Church, Heaven's own assayer,
Cast for dross the sanctuary's gold.

Shamed they look on her. But where her place is
    Christ's fair pleasances among,

PASQUEREL

Where with eyes of sister saints and faces
    Tender of archangels strong
Girt she goes, and the kind air untraces
Off her brows of maid the engraven wrong,

There, O even there, if, chance, up-blowing
    Out of earth remembrance ran
O'er her, soft she'll ponder in her going,
    Fallen a little moment wan,
Then the bright dews rain her overflowing
Heart of pity on despites of man.

BALLADS

BONNIE GRISELLE

A TALE OF 1715

'Peace, loud heart; wilt hinder me thou?
  Let me hear him, but hear:
Sure, Dickon's doublet is roomy enow;
  Oh, peace! for he's near.
It is Death riding post in the moon and the
    shadow,
And only a girl at the edge of a meadow
  Crying "stand" to him here.
Only a girl, but a girl can do;
Girl—and a sire to be saved thereto.'

Hist, hist, bonnie Griselle !
Listen it well,
Hoof of a galloper galloping nigher,
Sharp on the flint and soft in the mire,
Death at his saddlebow, bonnie Grisel

' " Win me but time," Lord Ronald sent wor
" Ere headsman go to 't ;
Time, but a week, for a cause reheard,
For a pardon afoot."
Staunch Lord Ronald and true Sir Harry
Much they can, will the axe but tarry
Till is pleaded the suit :
But oh, 'tis a head at the morning's light
If yonder letter win past to-night.'

Hist, hist, bonnie Griselle !
Listen it well,

BONNIE GRISELLE

Hoof of a galloper galloping nigher,

Death riding up for a sire, a sire,

And who to cry 'stand' but his bonnie Griselle?

'Cocked and primed be the two, no fear.

   (Ah, Heaven! if I fail.)

One to tumble him, one at his ear

   While I grope for the mail.

But, O if the bullet I meant but to stay him,

In the night and the fright go nearer and lay

   him

   Stone-deaf to my hail,

Blood on his breast, and his eye's dead stare,

How a girl in a doublet could murder there!'

   Hist, hist, bonnie Griselle!

     Listen it well,

Hoof of a galloper galloping nigher

To the dip o' the road and the musk-rose
    brier,

Hush! and the muzzle of bonnie Griselle.

'What have I done, kind Heaven, that I

    This horror must do?

Innocent hand, shall a poor knave die

    By malice of you?

White, white hand, art a-shaking already

At stain of the blood. Ah! for pity be steady

    Else worse is to rue.

Hand of his child, wilt fear to be red?

Coward!—a father will bleed in his stead.

    Hist, hist, bonnie Griselle!

      Wait for him well,

BONNIE GRISELLE

Hoof of the galloper nigher, oh, nigher.
Stand to it, child : it is death if the flier
Win by the watch of the bonnie Griselle.

'Shame ! I 'll dare it. Dear heart, and he 's near :
    Stand fast for the blow.
Yes, yes, at the oak, as the bridle leaps clear,
    Pull trigger. . . . Ah ! no.
Why is it I and not Dickon my brother,
Kind God, that must do it ?   Some other, some
        other
    Way save him than so !
But ah ! the grey eyes, if I fear to shoot,
And dear cheek I fondled—O father, I 'll do 't.'

    Fast, fast, bonnie Griselle !
        Cover him well,

Hoof coming on, coming on to the brier :

Pale is your face, but your heart is a fire :

Up in the moonlight ! ho ! bonnie Griselle.

   .   .   .   .   .

' Missed ! God help us ! . . . Ah ! no, for he's
    thrown. . . .

    Man, stir not a finger ;

'Tis a foot on your throat, and your brain out-
    blown

    Ere ye'd reach to your whinger. . . .

Mine's your letter, and thine's your life.

There. . . . Go comfort your wife, your wife,

    Good yeoman, and bring her

News of a rogue ye were stopped by—and tell

There's a brave knight the more for his daughter
    Griselle.'

BONNIE GRISELLE

Stand ho !   Cochrane's Griselle,
    Look at us well,
Lift us your face at the hoof coming nigher,
White as the moon but its eyes on a fire,
—And moonlight in love with the bonnie
    Griselle.

BALLADS

ON A BATTLEFIELD

SLATIN PASHA, AT FIRKET, JUNE 7, 1896

THE wheel of the world runs round amain :
　For who meet here by the moon, and how ?
Is it I the rider, and you the slain
　That were the slave and his lords but now ?
The wheel runs round in her circle true,
　The thrall aloft and the lords are under,
On the horseback I, at the horsehoof you.
　Stare, dead eyes, at your fortune's wonder !

　　Warily ho ! good Kismet, tread :
　　Thou and these of one wild are bred :
　　Wouldst not trample a kinsman's head.

ON A BATTLEFIELD

Wake, look up from the heap's edge there,
  Look at me, Turban Green, and know.
'Tis the barefoot slave at the Kaliph's chair,
  Who bore the flouting and feared the blow.
At the Kaliph's chair I marked your smile,
  And a bow-string pricks at my throat to think it.
Fate was filling her cup the while :
  'Tis I that mingle and you that drink it.

      Statelier go, stout Kismet, by :
      Lofty are low and the fallen high :
      At the horsehoof these, on the horseback I.

The wheel ran up and the wheel runs round
  To a victor's wail, to a captive's laughter :
It swings the scorner again to ground,
  The thrall to the thronèd moon.—And after ?

—Sleep, wild hearts, as our angers sleep,
   Till the rolling wheel that has dipped you under
Roll you up out of the dreamless deep,
   From the night's dismay to a daybreak's wonder.

      Softlier go, strong Kismet, past:
      The wheel of the world runs fast and fast:
      Who shall ride it on height at last?

DEATH'S DOOR

A BALLAD OF THE BIRKENHEAD

THE LAST AT CAPRERA

ENGLAND'S EYE

ON THE BRIDGE WITH THE ADMIRAL

AN UNDELIVERED LETTER

BALLADS

A BALLAD OF THE BIRKENHEAD

ALEXANDER CUMMINE RUSSELL.   DIED FEBRUARY 26,

1852

SHE settles at the prow.   (Hold off
  Our boat : the swirl would sink us, men,
When down the great ship goes.   Enough.)
  Dear Charlie, there he waves again.
My voice it is must sound his knell
In the grey English hall, and tell
How wofully they died and well.

Why am I safe, not there among
  My messmates ?   Soldiers ask not why :
We take our orders.   It was young
  At seventeen, they thought, to die.

DEATH'S DOOR

To die.   God, if 'twere only so!
One does not fear to drown : but O
Those devil-teeth agape below.

What is she thinking, Donald's wife
   Beside me, kirtling up her eyes?
Ah me! We save the helpless life
   And childish, but the strong man dies.
Let be : the flag had else a stain,
And all the glorious battle-rain
Could never wash it clear again.

I live to fight for it.   O yes,
   And see my bonnie North once more,
Home with the firs, the fells ; and press
   The blossomed heather.   (Ease the oar,
Men, watch it out : it soon will be.)
Yes, home, and at the gateward tree
Her face—O she'll be glad of me.

How steady on the sinking plank
  Our Seventy-fourth !   And I must miss
The praise of those who kept the rank,
  In England when they speak of this.
Steady as when it pipes to drill :
Ah no, but mute and stern and still,
As if the foe came up the hill.

Down !   She is gone.   How shake the
    deeps !
(Stand by to take some swimmer in.
No room ?   The pity !)   Lord, it creeps,
  The live sea creeps with nose and fin
And fang upswarming.   Ho ! 'tis good
Scot Donald yonder fights the flood.
God's   name !   they   must   not   have   his
    blood.

DEATH'S DOOR

(One more, we sink?)   And here by me
   She sits : and two months wedded.   No !
Part man and wife, it cannot be :
   No room by her?   I 'll make it—So.

.   .   .   .   .

(Give him a hand up there.   Good-bye.)
I watched the Seventy-fourth too nigh :
I could not live and let him die.

THE LAST AT CAPRERA

'COM'E ALLEGRO !'
(Garibaldi's last words.)

SILENT all an hour he lies,
   Being near to part,
Lion-leader mine ; his eyes
   Bent the sill athwart,

Watching, while his sands may run,
Ocean's breast, the chainless one ;
Watching beat against the sun
   Freedom's heart.

Shadow of a bird on air,
 Sound of wings alit !
Something on his face of rare
 Shone, beholding it.
Bird ? Ah, no ! That waning sight
Parleys, sure, with faery wight,
Herald of the mortal night
   Ere he flit.

Hist ! No look—ere charm he break
 Doom's light harbinger,
All as plain as if they spake
 Holding commune here.

DEATH'S DOOR

'Tis the boy that near his side
On Volturno as he died
Kissed the birthright earth in pride
    Slain for her.

Sudden—O from silence rang
   Speech! Was carol e'er,
Were it bird or sprite who sang,
   Joy-becharmed as there?
Strained the live heart thro' the throat,
Overwhelming note with note,
Till the headlong jubilance smote
    Rapt the air.

All as sudden it was done.
   Then with half his breath
Speaks the Chief. 'Ah, joyous one!
   Hear the joy,' he saith:

'He will have me forth with him.
Ah, the joy!' And, instant dim,
Eye and ear and voice and limb
    Slept the death.

This in death I loathe that he
    Shames a man,—to mark
How He binds like knave the free,
    Girds with caitiff sark.
Death the doomsman, him I hate,
Dragging man's reluctant weight
Like a felon from day's gate
    Down to dark.

So for me, if I must die
    On the sick man's down,

DEATH'S DOOR

When the war's forgot and I
   Spent and past renown;
If I may not fall afire
With the stormer's shout, or nigher
By the walls' heaped foot, or higher
      On their crown;

Then with Death would I cross hand,
   This my leader's way,
Joyous,—as when waiting stand
   Comrades of old fray,
Till its spoil the prison door
Loth to friend and cause give o'er,
And on Freedom's own once more
      Shines her day.

BALLADS

ENGLAND'S EYE

LIEUTENANT RAWSON, R.N., GUIDE OF THE ARMY
TO TEL-EL-KEBIR, SEPTEMBER 13, 1882

I

'SAILOR,' cried the Chief to me,
    Me of all his battle-band,
'You that steer a ship by sea,
    Will you steer a host by land?'
Then I pondered seconds twain,
    'There is sea-way wide and good,
    On the sand as on the flood,
And the stars are all as plain.'

DEATH'S DOOR

So this sailor answered, ' Ay,'
Frank and steady.   That is why
He to-night is England's Eye,
    None but he.

II

None but he !   For, bared to smite,
    England's sword comes onward blind,
Till the seaman aim it right :
    Sword shall fall, if eye shall find.
None but he !   The league of men
    At my lifted finger swerves
    This way, that : the steely curves
Straighten to the mark again.
    Seaman, find !   And, lo ! my star,
    Where the rebel ramparts are,
    Globed above our goal of war
        Lamps the fight.

III

Find it, seaman, find : for now
    Of a nation marching here
Pride will tower, or pride will bow,
    As thou prosper shalt or err.
Fortune of an empire forward
    Ranging by this bridle steers :
    O'er my sorrel's nodding ears
Stares the gaze of England warward.
    'Twixt a midnight and a morn,
    Till yon stars are overworn,
    England, on this saddle borne,
        Ridest Thou.

IV

I am I no more, but grown
    England : and her sailor she.

DEATH'S DOOR

High, beat higher, heart, and own
  Millionfold the pulse of me.
Long, O golden hour, be long.
    Ah, from this to fall again
    To the level ranks of men,
To the thousands of the throng !
    Once, on saddle or on ship,
    Once can Fate to mortal lip
    Press so rare a wine to sip,
      Once alone.

v

Ha ! what was it there upstole,
    Heaped against the glimmering lift ?
Faithful star ! the goal, the goal,
    In our vanward's very drift.

Mute the drowsy ramparts hang,
    See we grip them square and due.
    'Chief, and did I steer you true?'
    .   .   .   .   .

Off the rampart shook and sang
    Battle's startled wing in air,
Smote the breast, whom England there
'Twixt a dark and dawn to bear
    Gave her soul.

DEATH'S DOOR

ON THE BRIDGE WITH THE ADMIRAL

H.M.S. 'VICTORIA.' JUNE 22, 1893

SAVED.   She floats—if she'll but stay.
They'll not lose their sailor, they,
Admiral Lanyon, yet one day.

Near enough to sinking, though :
Would have sunk a rock, yon blow !
Stars ! what ailed him signal so ?

Something ailed him, sure, the best
Seaman on salt water.   Pest !
How they'll look and talk, the rest.

Can one lead and never blunder?
Yet to live this down! I wonder,
Would he grudge if he went under?

There he's waiting with set lip,
Mute, but saying to his ship
'Friend, together—if you dip.'

And he gave me once his eye:
Kind and plain as speech went by
Such a glance. His man am I.

Just a glance it was, and yet—
Well, 'twas his; and that's a debt
Shames a sailor to forget.

.   .   .   .   .

Ha! she lists! (is that the cry?)
Lists again to starboard. Why,
Then 'tis leap in time or die.

DEATH'S DOOR

Leap it is or drown, no third.
What's he thinking?   Has he heard,
That he lingers with the word?

No, 'tis coming now.   'The blame
All is mine.'   (The look that came
Through him of 'good-bye, the name'!)

'Save yourselves, men; each for each.'
Shall I, shall I?   There's no breach,
When the promise had no speech.

Each for each: and time to swim.
Why, 'twere dying for a whim,
If I stand and drown with him.

And the folk at home, they call
In my heart: if this befall,
Where's their boy the Admiral?

He's my friend, though, he, till this
Ended all : that glance of his
Signalled it too plain to miss.

Gone the rest.　The bridge is clear.
'Boy, what keeps you waiting here?'
Can one speak it to his ear?

He's my friend; his luck is flown.
That's the reason why his own
Cannot leave him die alone.

'Boy, she's going.'　Sir, I knew ;
But we stand by her, we two.
. . . No, sir, no.　I stay with you.

Boy and seaman, troth ye keep,
Not divided, all the deep
Whispering of how well ye sleep.

DEATH'S DOOR

AN UNDELIVERED LETTER

'On the cessation of the firing the Matabele approached closer, and found the Englishmen, most of whom were wounded, writing farewell messages to their relatives and friends. The Matabele then charged . . . all was soon over.'— *Times*, February 1894.

' SWEETHEART—for their fire is over,
  And a moment's grace they lend us
  Ere the savage spring and end us—
Here 's the last word from a lover.
  Who will bear it ?   Left alive
  Of our forty—'tis but five.

How we fought the black king, how
  Chased, you heard.   The river rose,
  Trapped us, river of the foes,
(Nay, my girl, 'tis England's now !)

Trapped, an arm's-length off our friends.
Then they closed : and here it ends.

Brother Dick's beside the mare.
Long the dead friend fenced him true
'Gainst the balls.   Now sleep the two
Cheek by cheek : I laid him there.
Let me spend six charges when
Comes the rush : I 'll join him then.

Here 's a blood-spot : dear, forgive.
All my blood for England's sake
Would I spill, nor grudge the stake :
But, for yours, 'twere sweet to live.

.   .   .   .   .

Ha ! they 're coming.   There—my kiss.
And God keep you after this.

BY WOOD AND WAVE

I

'The cradle of our race.' O where,
　　Lies nursing-lap of cradling hills,
Brother, like ours? So bland on air
　　Yon tender upland rim fulfils
With sweet outwandering and return
The slumber-dedicated urn.

II

A hollow land, she lies and hears
　　The storm-fit roar itself away
Beyond her; and for robe she wears,
　　If golden be the heaven or grey,
Through moods of mellow variance yet
One fashion of the violet.

BY WOOD AND WAVE

III

Wood waves from answering height to wood,
   And dove can echo wood-dove's note
With tidings of a sister's brood.
   On matin-dusk and vesper float
The pilgrim herons, ferrying o'er
The gulf of leafy shore and shore.

IV

And rolling a mute wave between,
   Deep-hearted, glassy-bosomed, wan,
In cloister of his willow-screen
   Revolving older things than Man,
The river-god goes darkling past,
A muffled sage, and fancy-fast.

V

see ! for where his slumbering brim
reaks in slope eddies huddling down
ir rockier bed, and watching him
rey turrets the soft headland crown,
re on his stair he turned and shone
oment's greeting, and is gone.

VI

ᴣ dwelt our fathers, ruling well
ıeir slender valley-kingdom's trust,
brief a line nor memorable,
ıt unreproached ; each tranquil, just
orial dynast, sire to son,
ding the unstoried sceptre on.

BY WOOD AND WAVE

To them the Song-Muse wandered not,
　　Or slumbered, if she came,—so soft
Our meadows,—and her quest forgot.
　　Nor flying Fame lit here : aloft
She crossed their hilltops like the breeze,
Nor spied them, lost among their trees.

O fameless plenitude of days,
　　Meek honour of a steadfast house,
If mortal steadfastness be praise
　　Ours were not all inglorious :
She stood not idly, standing sure ;
Some glory is it to endure.

NOSTRÆ INCUNABULA GENTIS

IX

Ah, me ! this gentle namesake earth
　　Breathed glory for her brood : she spoke
Of nursing-dues her children's worth
　　Upgrown should render : witching broke
Across this upland bourne of home
The landscape of a deed to come.

X

There breathes from her a glory now
　　For dreamer in home's haunted wood :
There drops wild honey from the bough,
　　Old raptures of the childish blood ;
And all the leafy whisper sighs
With gust of boyhood's chivalries.

A HIGHLAND RIVER

From the wild whereout I ran,
Purple gates of Grampian,
Down the boon land wander I,
Amuinn, rejoicingly.
Here the mild wood-shadows fall
And the wood-notes musical.
Here the white-throat ouzel skims,
Where the rapid foams and dims,
Dims and foams, from shoal to pool,
Pool to shallow ; and the cool,
Amber under-waves embrace
Silken fin and silvern lace
Of the sea-drove upward steering.
Or at times the red cliffs nearing

A HIGHLAND RIVER

owd my echoing flood between,

ıd in cleft or ivy screen

:mpt the harbouring dove to build,

· the daws' complaining guild.

llying then by meads I run

oadening in the embracing sun ;

ll that winsome mountain elf,

ıne, and talking to himself

· the leaning alder copse,

om the far moss cradle drops,

air by pebbly stair, the burn.

· in lonest reach the hern

: the wanderer's foot aware

ıuses him and climbs the air,

ıred on fanning wings away

ll he mingles, grey in grey.

BY WOOD AND WAVE

NEW YEAR IN THE SOUTH

I

THE South breathes up from yonder sea
  And on her wings the noon :
Earth heaves her bosom winter-free
  As if the Yule were June.

From quickening briar and flower unrolled
  Climbs hitherward the South,
By bowers that hold the fruit of gold
  To hill-woods red with drouth.

The olives on the mountain knees
  Have dreamt that summer came,
And, kindled at the fanning breeze,
  Break silverly aflame.

Yon cypress, blackening in the beam
  That lights the grave he mourns,
Folds darklier yet his shrouds of jet,
  But, in their darkness, burns.

70

NEW YEAR IN THE SOUTH

The heaven has joy, and joy the earth.
  O Soul, and what hast thou?
What part is thy part in the mirth
  From wave to mountain brow?
Is rather thine the mood of tears,
  Of mortal tears, that stir
In whom the immortal Beauty nears
  And meets no mate for her:
On whom her dawn of splendour rolls
  And lights him but for this—
To measure and to mourn the soul's
  Incompetence of bliss:
Who reaches where her skirts have been,
  And, reaching, comes no nigher,
Such deep unseen doth sleep between
  Man's flesh and man's desire?

III

Ah, Soul! not so the deep divides
　But thine are kindred there:
This Joy in holy pageant rides
　To lift thee to her chair.
A wanderer out of worlds forgot
　Thou bear'st the birthright mind:
Look where thine own forget thee not,
　Spirit, and know thy kind.
Thou mournest but as exiles may
　Their yet unlifted ban;
Feelest the pang of heaven's estray,
　The home-woe of the man:
An isle-pent watcher sights afar
　Some ranger of the foam,
And weeping hails o'er broadening sails
　The pennon of his home.

NEW YEAR IN THE NORTH

I

FROM Eastland comes the white Year up,
   A golden sun he bears,
As priest that lifts a shining cup
   Along heaven's altar stairs.
His bright robe-fringes trailing wide
   Let float their purple fret,
To flush old Grampian's umbered side
   And brows of violet.
His eyes have seen in mirror sheen
   The sparkle of his crown,
Where Amuinn foams her pines between,
   And plainward wandering down,

73

Forgets the inurning height that stores
  The silence of her glen,
To babble laughter at the doors,
  Or rouse the mills of men.

II

Fair stream that goest from glen to lea
  So strongly and so glad—
Life's river might it flow like thee,
  Strong, and with beauty clad !
Yon sunlight of the dawning year
  On thy pure bosom strown,
Might beam of it be glassed as clear,
  Blithe Amuinn, on mine own !
As 'neath the glow descends thy flow
  From hills of virgin air
To service and to song below,
  Ah ! let my life-flow fare,

NEW YEAR IN THE NORTH

To charm asleep one hungerer's need,
   To lull one mourner's wrong,
With doer's music of a deed,
   Or singer's deed of song.

III

Doer or Singer—must man choose?
   Must time's brief children swear
Sole fealty, and the jealous muse
   Love only or forbear?
Kind First-foot on my pathway borne,
   Speak: to thy rede I bow:
What counsel on the all-omened morn,
   Wise Amuinn, spellest thou?
Thou answerest, 'Where my currents fleet
   And where mine echoes throng,
There voice and work are one, the sweet
   Is gendered of the strong.

And, Singer, thou let service breed
  Music that serves again ;
And song-breath speed the golden deed
  That coins man's heart for men.'

A HOME REVISITED

I TREAD the shorn and windy heath
　　That sees the latest daylight fail,
The wide blue vapour swims beneath
　　And fills the warm lap of the vale,
From far-off meadow-pastures dim
To yon lone scar's enfolding rim.

From distance to this airy place
　　Mounts up the thunder of the fall,
Where, taking voice a moment-space,
　　And whitening o'er his barrier-wall,
From deep above to deep below
Moves the strong Avon's urgent flow.

BY WOOD AND WAVE

And all between high crag and wave
  A wealth of happy woodland springs,
With beechen cloisters mute and grave,
  Or brakes astir with sunny wings,
Or, fast in ivy-curtained sleep,
Some boulder tumbled from the steep.

But oh! the red-trunked pines that rear
  Broad limbs against the sunset flame,
Whence nightly to my childish ear
  The wood-dove's cradle-music came,
Till fell the lid on dreaming eye,
And with her in the woods was I.

Dear voice of home, I hearken, lo!
  A child once more; the hot years roll
Their burden off: again I know
  The twilight of the dawning soul;

A HOME REVISITED

Kind sylvan, chant : nor start to hear
A foster-brother's footfall near.

For while I listen darkly swell
   Old yearnings dumb of home and kind ;
But early on my soul they fell,
   And now, as then, no language find.
Speak thou, dear voice of home, and be
My speechless longing voiced in thee.

'THE OCEAN THRONE'

CHORIC SONGS FROM A MASQUE
WRITTEN FOR MUSIC AND PERFORMED AT THE CELE-
BRATION OF THE FIFTIETH YEAR OF THE REIGN OF
QUEEN VICTORIA

F

COUNTRYMEN

Our herds roam wide by covert-side,
Through meadows which the oaks bestride
   To shade the red kine under,
Where dumb and dark the river crawls,
Or girds against his foaming walls
   And volleys down in thunder.
Our white flocks star the pastures, hung
The dimpled woods and knolls among;
   The fleeces climb and glimmer,
From musky dells of brier and bine
To where the grey down-grasses shine
   Bare in the noonday shimmer.

THE OCEAN THRONE

Our steady ploughs on wold and plain
Go marching, with the swarthy train
  Of rooks that hover leeward;
Go tasting deep the oozy lea
Whence out we drove the northern sea
  And scared the gannet seaward.
And o'er us all, on•farm and hall,
In peace the mellow summers fall,
  In peace their dole outmeasure;
Nor alien's war, nor brothers' jar
Can shake our settled calm and mar
  The girdled island's treasure.

MINERS AND CRAFTSMEN

MINERS AND CRAFTSMEN

WITH tick and click of groping pick
We furrow the womb of darkness thick,
   In the deep mine's reek and smother;
With drills that drive and blasts that rive,
We burrow the cells of the grimy hive
   With labour and swink and pother:
And the lantern's glare we shelter ware,
Lest the fire-fiend rise from his roky lair
   On blue bat-pinion sailing,
And the thunder clap of his wing's wide flap
A township's best in ruin enwrap,
   And the wives above stand wailing.

85

THE OCEAN THRONE

But save we toil in the vaulted hill
The labouring wheels of the world were still,
 To dust and rust returning;
By us the wingless navies glide
Vapour-winged on a windless tide;
 The sounding mills go churning;
With whir and boom, through glint and gloom,
The dancing shuttle athwart the loom
 The nimble thread up-snatches;
And flung from torturing furnace womb
The live white ores in fury fume
 Through torrent-roaring hatches.

THE GENTLE

WE come from tower and grange,
Where the grey woodlands range,
Folding chivalric halls in ancient ease ;
From Erin's rain-wet rocks,
Or where the ocean-shocks
Thunder between the glimmering Hebrides ;
And many-spired cities grave,
With terraced riverain hoar lapped by the
storied wave.

Taught in proud England's school,
Her honour's knightly rule,
To do and dare and bear and not to lie,
With priest's or scholar's lore,
Or statesman's subtle store

THE OCEAN THRONE

Of garnered wisdom, proved in councils high,
We serve thy bidding here, or far
Shepherd the imperial flock under an alien star.

Leechcraft of heaven or earth
We bear to scanted hearth
And lightless doorway and dim beds of pain :
With master-craft we steer
Dusk labour's march, and cheer
His blind innumerable-handed train ;
Or in the cannon-shaken air
Frankly the gentle die that simple men may dare.

The Asian moonbeams fall
O'er our boys' graves, and all
The o'er-watching hills are names of their
young glory :
Sleep the blithe swordsman hands
Beside red Æthiop sands,

Or drear uprise of wintry promontory :
The headstone of a hero slain
Charms with his memory's spell each threshold of
thy reign.

O for the blood that fell
So gladly given and well,
O for all spirits that lived for England's
honour,
Ere folly ruin or fear
Her whom these held so dear,
Ere fate or treason shame the crown upon
her,
Rise, brothers of her knightly roll,
Close fast our order's ranks and guard great
England whole.

SOLDIERS

I

Lads that love fight,
Hearts that beat right,
Rally ho! rally, and lock the rank tight:
Scarlet or blue,
Tartan and trew,
Fit to go anywhere, anything do.
Rings with our tramp,
Glows with our camp
Jungle or wady or prairie or swamp;
Shipboard or shore,
Climates a score,
Burning dust-desert or Himalay hoar.

SOLDIERS

Bids us to war,

Mahdi or Czar,

War shall not tarry where Englishmen are.

Home they go tame,

Headlong who came,

Fire-footed Arab and Ghazi aflame.

Flout they our sway

Long worlds away,

Longer the arm is we reach to the prey:

Forest and hill

Crossed we at will,

Hunting the thieves of the Sùleiman chill:

Where the south land

Burns like a brand,

Climbed the tall side of the ship of the sand;

Bridled the staid

Nubian jade,

Stalking to battle in gaunt cavalcade.

THE OCEAN THRONE

Heard our 'heave-ho!'

Watched the oars go

Ghosts of grey Pharaohs and idols a-row;

Mile by long mile

Beat we old Nile.

Where are they safe from the men of the Isle?

II

Ha! for how we

Shook ourselves free,

Leapt to fetch Gordon safe home over sea.

What! shall a debt

England forget?

We, we will pay it, clasp hands with him yet.

Silent and stark,

Sheer at their mark,

Strode our scant thousand out into the dark:

SOLDIERS

Tempted the dread

Pathways that thread

Realms of the vulture, mute camps of the dead :

Shook the wild hive,

Let the swarm drive,

Myriad stings of that hurricane live ;

Let the storm fall,

Moved like a wall

Into it, out of it, safe——Ah ! not all.

Hollow their grave,

Heroes who gave

Life for the hero it helped not to save ;

Smooth the lone bier ;

Peace ! dry the tear :

Hand shall clasp hand, but not here, O not here.

SAILORS

I

Sailors we, the island breed,

Merry sons of stout sea-rover;

Merry hearts and tough at need;

Who like us wide ocean over?

South or north

Steering forth

Where's the sea but England sailed it?

East or west,

Where's the quest

Asked a man, and England failed it?

Over tides that sleep or rave,

Ocean old, the islesmen know you:

Bellow wind and buffet wave,

We're the hearts will overcrow you.

SAILORS

Chorus

When the storm in sheet and shroud
    Blusters loud,
When the rollers shake the decks,
    Rolling wrecks,
O it's who will show the way
    Up the roaring mast to-day,
O it's who but merry seamen of the Isle?

II

Hearts of oak, our sires, who knew
    Nelson's snowy towers upsoaring,
Strangelier ride our Jackets Blue,
    Strange sea-horses weirdly oaring.
        Under us snort
        Fire-fed, swart,

THE OCEAN THRONE

Foaming-finned Behemoths wallowing,

Dragon scale,

Hump of mail,

Sunken nozzle the sea-mound hollowing.

Beam of oak or beam of steel,

Hearts of oak are the men that ride
them;

England's war-dogs dour and leal

Guard her folds lest harm betide them.

Chorus

When the slaver were-wolf creeps,

Ere he leaps:

When the pirate hawk a-stoop

Thinks to swoop:

O the vermin flit and fly,

For it's who, it's who they spy,

O it's who but merry seamen of the Isle?

SAILORS

Fighters we, the Viking seed,
　　By the flagship staunchly steering,
Trimly dight for murderous deed,
　　Broadside slow to broadside nearing.
　　　　Battle's breath,
　　　　A sword in sheath,
Waits the grim word long withholden:
　　　　Through the hush
　　　　O'er us rush
Dreams of home and summers golden.
　　Sword　from　sheath,　the　lightning
　　　　springs,
　　Flap the enormous wings of thunder:
All the bruised heaven reels and rings,
　　Quail the torn, white surges under.

THE OCEAN THRONE

Chorus

Then my messmate's eyes by mine
    Starkly shine,
In the gun-fire's moment fit
    Fiercely lit;
And it's who will show the way
Through the pelting fight to-day,
O it's who but merry seamen of the Isle?

THE MOTHER AND THE SONS

1

Sons in my gates of the West,
Where the long tides foam in the dark of the
    pine,
And the cornlands crowd to the dim sky-line,
And wide as the air are the meadows of kine,
    What cheer from my gates of the West?

' Peace in thy gates of the West,
    England our mother, and rest,
In our sounding channels and headlands frore
The hot Norse blood of the northland hoar
Is lord of the wave as the lords of yore,
    Guarding thy gates of the West.

THE OCEAN THRONE

But thou, O mother, be strong
　In thy seas for a girdle of towers,
Holding thine own from wrong,
　Thine own that is ours.
Till the sons that are bone of thy bone,
Till the brood of the lion upgrown
　In a day not long,
Shall war for our England's own,
For the pride of the ocean throne,
　Be strong, O mother, be strong.'

II

Sons in my gates of the morn,
That steward the measureless harvest gold
And temples and towers of the Orient old
From the seas of the palm to Himálya cold,
　What cheer in my gates of the morn ?

THE MOTHER AND THE SONS

' Fair as our India's morn

Thy peace, as a sunrise, is born.

Where thy banner is broad in the Orient light

There is law from the seas to Himálya's height,

For the banner of might is the banner of right.

Good cheer in thy gates of the morn.'

III

From the isles of the South what word?

Gallant sons of the South! for that trumpet rang
    high,

When 'England's are ours' was the gathering-
    cry,

'And a thousand will bleed ere our Gordon shall
    die.'

From my sons of the South what word?

THE OCEAN THRONE

'Mother, what need of a word
  For the love that outspoke with the
    sword?
In the day of thy storm, in the clash of the
    powers,
When thy children close round thee grown great
    with the hours,
They shall know who have wronged thee if
    "England's be ours."
We bring thee a deed for a word.

But thou, O mother, be strong
  In thy seas for a girdle of towers,
Holding thine own from wrong,
  Thine own that is ours.
Till the sons that are bone of thy bone,
Till the brood of the lion upgrown

THE MOTHER AND THE SONS

In a day not long,
Shall war for our England's own,
For the pride of the ocean throne,
Be strong, O mother, be strong.'

'THE CLOUD OF MORTAL DESTINY'

A DEATH IN THE MIST

A STAR IN THE EAST

LOVE THE TIMELESS

REWARD

TO A LEADER

THE ANGEL STAIR

A DEATH IN THE MIST

'CLOUD and for ever cloud
Round me, with floor of an unending snow,
Where all ways are alike to all, and go
    Only from shroud to shroud,
As melt the formless arches and upgrow
    In vapour-crypts embowed.

And some one in the vale
Opens at morn his casement, if the morn
Be risen below, and sweeps with glances worn
    The mountain knees, and pale
Rain-soaken pastures hung with fringes torn
    Of my death-curtain's trail.

THE CLOUD OF MORTAL DESTINY

And wonders how his friend
Brooks the sad tarriance in the mountain cot,
So long by leaguer of the mists, that blot
    The skyward stairway, penned;
And moving faintlier in my moving grot
    I, while he wonders, end.

    Cloud!   In the cloud to die!
Alas! as ever in the cloud I lived.
Where   trod   these   feet,   undoubting?   where
    achieved
    One of all goals that lie
Sun-clear to those who lightlier have believed,
    Not keenlier gazed than I?

    Bright action's train I viewed
Hungering, afar; nor followed, for disdain

A DEATH IN THE MIST

To sell the heart to serve and not the brain.
    Truth the divine I wooed
Long, and a changeling bride to breast I strain,
    Divine Incertitude.

    Divine—or I misdeemed :
So holier was my bosom-mate to me,
This blind, this mortal, but no phantom she,
    Than ghostlier Fair that beamed
Glamour on easier lovers, fain to be
    Blest but the while they dreamed.

    Not dream would I, to wake
Fooled, if a waking be ; nor dream, to sleep
On past reproof of folly, if the deep
    Shall whom it sent retake,
Nor over that strict edge one memory creep,
    When the fond senses break.

THE CLOUD OF MORTAL DESTINY

Then since I could not know,
And dream I would not, in my cloudy pall
I wander, where all ways are like, and all
Into one blankness go :
I find no faith with warrant for her call,
No battle worth my blow.

Ah, me ! perchance the while,
Heaven-plain above the darkness where I drown,
The changeless towers of the white Alpine crown,
Crystalline pile and pile,
Out of eternal clearness shining down
On the lost mortal smile.'

.   .   .   .   .

Breath of the North and broad
Noon heaven : a wanderer prone along the drift,

A DEATH IN THE MIST

Cold ; and he knew not o'er the mountain clift
    How leapt a wind and trod
His darkness out, and showed on stainless lift
    The steadfast towers of God.

A STAR IN THE EAST

THE boy whose dreaming eye discerns
   On life's far verge a glory seen,
And knows his star arisen, and burns
   To tread the width of world between—
How starts he at that passion's birth,
   In those lit eyes what visions swim !
Above, beneath, new heaven, new earth ;
   And all things round one heart with him.

Ah ! drink, young dreamer, of thy joy,
   Drink deeply now, nor taste again :
So soon the manhood mocks the boy,
   So scant the fruit, so large the pain ;

A STAR IN THE EAST

So sure a doubt the vision hides,
    Faint and more faint, the more pursued;
So far the broadening world divides
    Thy passion and the star it wooed.

Yet, though the rapt hour come not back,
    Though faith's clear flame, which lit thee then,
Scarce gleam to show thy fading track
    Among the thousand ways of men:
Though one wide moment gave and stole
    The opening heaven, and left the cloud:
Though not again is born the soul,
    And once, but once, the life is vowed:

Yet, oh! brave heart that daredst to dream,
    Dare yet believe thy dreaming true,
Dare trust the star's remembered gleam,
    The trembling of the unfallen clue:

THE CLOUD OF MORTAL DESTINY

The rapt hour passes as it came,
  But passing sows the live desire :
Once on thy brows alit the flame,
  Now in thy bosom bides the fire.

And still through storm and wildering gloom,
  O'er sun-blanched waste, o'er oceans wan,
The deep unseen upholding doom
  Sweeps the soul's pinion strongly on ;
Till winged along the enchanted line
  The straining spirit nears the mark,
And, fainting, knows a hand divine
  Reach out and take it through the dark.

So, haply, gazing from the brows
  Of forests o'er the pathless foam,
Some bird of passage inly knows
  The pilot sense that steers her home :

A STAR IN THE EAST

And rustling from her shade of oak
    With clap of wing awakes the hush,
And joys in the strong sinew's stroke,
    And raptures at the breezes' rush :

Then buoyed along the constant deep,
    Or stemming true the ruffling gales,
With surely forward-faring sweep
    And soundless beat of pinion, sails :
Till downward through the sunset bloom
    She stoops, with one slow oar-beat more,
And lets descend a wearying plume
    At even on the island shore.

LOVE THE TIMELESS

ALL on a dawning rosy-dim
My soul woke, ere could wake a limb,
And 'tired herself and stole abroad.
There found she on a starward road
Some that were once her company.
Now who they were that met her I
Guess lightly, but of what was heard
From lip to lip I know no word.
For home she softly came unmissed,
Doffed her sky-faring robe, and kissed
To living sense her slumbering clay,
Told so much of her airy way,
No more; and smiling down my guess,
Back kissed me to forgetfulness.

. . . . .

LOVE THE TIMELESS

But not the less in slumber wrought
My questing mind. 'For how,' methought,
'Can commune be of clime and clime,
The timeless and the bound in time?
As soon might echoes cross, unbuoyed
On air's upholding waves, the void
And stayless, star-enisling deep,
As mortal thoughts, that measure keep
With crawling of the dial's hand
And lapses of the wasting sand,
Be syllabled on ears for whom
A moment spans an æon's room.
Deem we the spirit, that last ungirt
Earth's heavy raiment, in the skirt
And doubtful dusk of Time abides,
From portion in these human tides
Not yet so disinherited,
But parleyings of the quick and dead

THE CLOUD OF MORTAL DESTINY

May meet upon this pulse of air?
Ah, no! Time's sons are equal there;
Nor yonward of Death's instant gate
Is last or first, is soon or late.
The wings of all the ghostly flight
Together on God's threshold light
As one; nor earlier there are borne
Our fathers of grey Nature's morn
Than he whose spirit launched away
Down the dawn-wind of yesterday.'

Then seemed it from exceeding far,
As though a voice from off a star
Were blown me hither, came a word,
' O dull of heed, and hast not heard
How for all Being only Love
Was builder and is bond thereof?

LOVE THE TIMELESS

Her arms as in an urn enwall
The ocean of the shoreless All,
And ocean-isle of Space therein.
The worlds that end not nor begin,
The world that hears the hurrying breath
Of Time outmeting Birth and Death,
Both to one music's order move,—
The beating of the heart of Love.
Therefore whatso of Love is, may
'Twixt mortal and immortal day
Unhindered voyage and unspent,
Across Love's equal element.
And therefore, if some widowed sigh
Of mourner climb your vault of sky,
Hopeless, in hunger for the dead,
Or hearts in rest are visited,
Even they, with longing for their own,—
O then they hearken, leaning down

THE CLOUD OF MORTAL DESTINY

Over heaven's brim as o'er a cup,

The human murmur trembling up.

Their swift, unrhythmed, changeless Now

Stands still: the wan earth blinks below:

And Time is doled to spirits then

By clock-beat of the towers of men.

REWARD

REWARD

WHAT shall the brave in soul attain
  Who shape a thought in act and life,
What guerdon to redeem the pain,
  What victor palm beyond the strife,
When the worn spirits pass to wait
In silence with the silent great?

Men say, 'It were reward for all—
  For hours of strife an age of fame!'
Ah! faint, methinks, the echoes fall
  Of mortals' praise or mortals' blame,
When breaks upon the widening soul
The deep archangel trumpet-roll.

121

THE CLOUD OF MORTAL DESTINY

Nay, brothers, 'neath the Eternal Eyes
    One human joy shall touch the just,—
To know their spirit's heirs arise
    And lift their purpose from the dust;
The father's passion arms the son,
And the great deed goes on, goes on.

TO A LEADER

Lead on, strong heart, lead on untiring still,
  Though the day darken, and a wearier war,
  Wave after bitter wave, come rolling far,
  From seas undrainable of wasteful ill.
But thou lead on : thou shalt not vainly spill
  Thy heart's dear blood, but, fast as hate can
    mar,
  It quickens, fallen where God's harvests are,
  Round happier dwellings which thy children
    fill.
Lead on ; watch out the last, the blindest, fight ;
Watch out the trouble to watch in the weal,

123

THE CLOUD OF MORTAL DESTINY

This one last hour of battle : even now
Perchance, above us, from his vantage height
The angel watcher marks the foeman reel,
And sets the trumpet to his lips to blow.

THE ANGEL STAIR

MESEEMED upon a stair was I
That bridged the air's immensity,
   Mounting I saw not whence nor where,
So lost below, so lost on high :
   And a strong angel clomb the stair,
   And on his breast a soul he bare.

Hard at my side the angel set
A resting foot.   I knew, and yet
   Knew not the Still one, folded o'er,
Strange in dusk weed of violet :
   The travel-robe of saints he wore
   Which wraps them changing shore for shore.

THE CLOUD OF MORTAL DESTINY

A shepherd crook of sapling grain
He clasped, as who to sleep had lain
  Holding it, and the sleep was death.
White was the smooth brow, marble-plain.
  ' Thy years,' methought, ' of mortal breath
  Were His who taught from Nazareth.'

White was the dreaming brow, but white
As beam is of the live moonlight,
  Wherein the far sun mirrored lies.
' It falleth on him from the height '
  (The angel spake) ' whereto we rise,
  That shineth over Paradise.'

My lips unlocked, ' And is there dearth
In heaven, that this blossomed worth
  Ye pluck before to fruit it grew ? '
And mild he answered, ' On your earth

THE ANGEL STAIR

The Christ He worketh hitherto :
And His, that die, not cease to do.'

'Not less,' I said, 'but more were strong
That after-deed, if ours among .
    Longer his living footstep trod.'
And he, 'Your mortal brief and long
    How should I mete ?   Our angel rod
    Holds measure from the spans of God.'

'O Seraph, in the doom of soul
Is all as one Time's varying dole ?
    Life's wholeness as the tithe thereof ? '
'O Man, this tithe of life was whole.
    He chose,—that choice is written above.
    He loved,—what can ye more than love ? '

.   .   .   .   .

THE CLOUD OF MORTAL DESTINY

His mantle's rustle and the breath
Went past me like a sigh. . . . Beneath
   One sighed indeed, half risen from prayer.
For lo! it was the bed of death.
   Young brother, the white brow was there :
Thou—far upon the Angel Stair.

INSCRIPTIONS

FOR A STATUE IN A SCHOOL CHAPEL

THOSE eyes have lost their fires : the tool
    Not so could grave, or marble shine :
Thy Presence bears its olden rule
    Else, and yon scholar ranks are thine.

O strong and tender, even to-day
    Not the cold stone can quench thee so,
But folly shall his footstep stay,
    To look thee in the eyes, and know.

INSCRIPTIONS

ON A CENOTAPH IN A SCHOOL CHAPEL[1]

TO A. C. R.

THERE the wave urns thee deep: thine urn
  Here, comrade, is thy living deed.
Sleep in our midst, or waking learn
  That hero blood was hero seed.

TO A YOUNG BOY

YOUNG brother, is it risen so soon—
Thy star of eve, before thy noon?
The star of eve! Ah, care not thou:
God's morning shall be long enow.

[1] See 'Ballad of the Birkenhead,' p. 42.

A BRAVE PHYSICIAN

O WHO wouldst Honour for thine own
    And knightly Truth, come musing here,
And breathe a vow beside the stone
    That names our Knight Hospitaller.

TO SUSANNA

FAIR soul, who warest, pure of blame,
    Thy white life through, the Lily's name,
Wear now the flower of holier sod,
    The Lily of the Peace of God.

INSCRIPTIONS

'DULCES MORIENS REMINISCITUR ARGOS'

'FRIENDS—for death called and I knew—
Stoop; let me speak ere I pass;
Friends, when you carry me forth
And lay me low under the grass,
Grant, as I loved her, but this ;—
Lay what is left of me true
To the home where my heart was and is,
Lay me, my face to the North.'

Brother, loved brother and lost,
Tenderly lay we thee down.
There, from thy grave looking forth,
Work not, but watch, with thine own.
Ours while the battle was sore,
Keep, in the silence, thy post,
Ours till the battle is o'er,
Faithful, thy face to the North.

A CHOICE OF SOLOMON

AMONG the shadows of a dell
　　One mused upon his things to be,
　　For summers now a score had he.
There came a voice (he knew not well
If from the boughs or heaven it fell)
　　Said, 'Ask what I shall give to thee.'

Then he,—' A great one yesterday
　　Went up the long street girt about
　　With rapture of the people's shout.
But on his wreath a dew there lay,
And this was blood. Ah me ! the bay
　　Veiled ill the sick heart peering out.

137

A CHOICE OF SOLOMON

'And yester-eve I marked a sage
   Look upward on a star and sigh,
   As lovers use when none are by :
But he for lovelessness and age,
And the lone search to disengage
   Cold secrets of the careless sky.

'Not mine, bleak laurel plucked from wrong !
   Nor mine, harsh fruit yon searchers pull !
   Let days of mine flow scant or full,
But flow to music borne along.
Be wise who will, who will be strong :
   Give me that life be beautiful.

'O son,' was answered in the bower,
   'Because thou chosen hast for prize
   What nearest on Love's bosom lies,
Therefore shall Beauty be thy dower,

A CHOICE OF SOLOMON

And that thou hast not chosen, Power,
    And Wisdom wiser than the wise.

'For mystery shall ungird her cloud,
    To shine on selfless eyes that bear
    Her parleyings on the veilless air.
And bidden of thee shall bow the proud,
Unloth, nor witting if he bowed,
    Betrayed to goodness unaware.'

He woke. Behold, the shining noon
    Drank up the vision like the steam
    Of morn. And was the voice a stream
That muttered near, a wind's commune
With woodland? Ah! 'tis proven soon,
    Be dreamer true but as the dream.

AT LETHE'S BRINK

AT LETHE'S BRINK

WILLIAM EWART GLADSTONE AND PRINCE EDWARD OF
YORK, JUNE 1895

By Lethe wave that hems away
    Earth's murmur and the Elysian ease,
Here on this hither brink of day,
    What spirits strangely met be these :
One from that silence parted new,
The other with his face thereto ?

Grey statesman fondling on the knee
    A babbling prince and wordless yet,
O with what lore of rule can he
    Be lessoned, ere thyself forget ;

AT LETHE'S BRINK

Ere from the slumber-river's brink
He sunders, and 'tis thine to drink?

Bland infant, reaching palm to span
   Yon puissant brow where wisdom lies,
Lo! thrice a storied age of man
   Looks down from those world-reading eyes,
Yet never ray the more for this
Can light thy dawning orbs from his.

O Chief, that hast ungirt the care,
   O Child, that yet shalt wear thine own,
O Past and Future fronted there
   All knowing and with all unknown,
Ye stand at helpless gaze the while
In empty commune of a smile.

Yea, when did Past the Future teach?
   Life's fruits were viler, garnered so.

AT LETHE'S BRINK

We learn but what we live : and, each
  Worn harvester, we turn and go
Clasping in wistful bosom stored
Our incommunicable hoard.

A LULLABY TO A LYRE

REST, rest, weary my lyre,
  Passion her flight has soared.
Rest with her, rest ; let her wings of fire
  Droop by the drooping chord.
Cometh at last a sleep to the strong,
  Cometh a sleep to song,
    Cometh to song.

Dream, dream, airy my lyre,
  Cradled in fancy's glade :
Dream but how to a wind drawn nigher
  Answer a mavis made.

143

A LULLABY TO A LYRE

Music of bower and bird shall be
Music, O lyre, of thee,
Music of thee.

Sleep, sleep, merry my lyre.
Blithe from that easing spell
Nerve will tremble, and blithe respire
Breast of the sounding shell.
Passion will rouse at thy side once more,
Waken her wings and soar,
Waken and soar.

Printed by T. and A. Constable, Printers to Her Majesty
at the Edinburgh University Press